THIS IS THE ROOM WHERE **LIVES** SLIP AWAY **ONE** GRAIN AT A **TIME**...

1

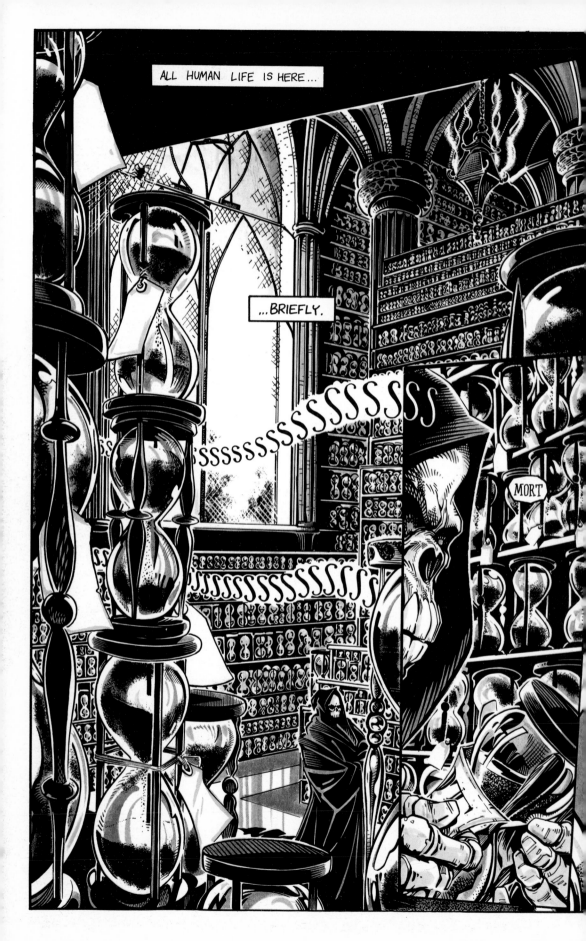

MORT

A Discworld Big Comic

TERRY PRATCHETT

Illustrated by
GRAHAM HIGGINS

VG GRAPHICS 1994

DEDICATIONS

TERRY:

One more for Rhianna

GRAHAM:

To Matthew and James,
who would like me to include
Bruce Grobelaar

2 001 064 759

First published in Great Britain 1994
by Victor Gollancz Ltd
A Division of the Cassell group
Villiers House, 41/47 Strand, London WC2N 5JE
First Gollancz Paperback edition 1994

Text © Terry and Lyn Pratchett 1994
Illustrations © Graham Higgins 1994
Coloured by Carol Bennett
Lettering by Euan Smith

Discworld® is a trade mark registered by Terry Pratchett.

A catalogue record for this book is available from the British Library.

The right of Terry Pratchett to be identified as author of this work, and of
Graham Higgins to be identified as the illustrator, has been asserted by them
in accordance with the Copyright, Designs and Patents Act, 1988.

ISBN 0 575 05697 5 (hardback)   ISBN 0 575 05699 1 (paperback)

Printed in Italy by New Interlitho Italia SpA

4

COME ON, LAD
HIRIN' DAY'S OVER
NOW.

NO! IT'S NOT
OVER UNTIL
MIDNIGHT

YOU'RE TOO
STUBBORN FOR YOUR
OWN GOOD, BOY...

IT'S A WORTHY JOB, UNDERTAKING...

UNDERTAKING? DAD, HE'S A SKEL...!

YOU WANT AN APPRENTICE?

IT'S MY BUSY TIME

...AND IT'S VERY... NECESSARY.

ER...AND I DON'T HAVE TO DIE?

BEING DEAD IS NOT COMPULSORY

AND... AND THE BONES?

NOT IF YOU DON'T WANT TO

WHAT ABOUT THE HORSE?

IT GOES WITH THE JOB

YES!

10

JUST A SPLASH OF LAVENDER WATER MY GOOD MAN

13

15

THAT'S **STUPID**, BOY. APPRENTICES BECOME **MASTER**, AND YOU CAN'T...

MORT, MY NAME IS **MORT**.

I'D HAVE EXPECTED SOMETHING LIKE **FANG** OR **FURY**.

BINKY'S A NICE NAME

YOU'VE MET MY **DAUGHTER**?

OH YES, SIR.

SHE LIKES TO HAVE SOMEONE HER OWN AGE TO TALK TO

I'M SURE YOU'LL GET ALONG LIKE A **HOUSE** ON **FIRE**...

...THEY TASTE OF PEPPERMINT

oh

I'LL BE DAMNED

POSSIBLY, SIR

WHAT HAPPENS NEXT?

I DON'T KNOW. I'VE NEVER DIED

WHY AREN'T I ANGRY?

EMOTIONS GET LEFT BEHIND

I SUPPOSE THERE'S NO CHANCE..?

THERE'S NO CHANCE AT ALL

I KNOW YOU CAN HEAR ME

DON'T TRUST HIM

COME

she saw me

22

WHY DO YOU LET THAT SORT OF THING HAPPEN? YOU COULD HAVE STOPPED IT

I AM NOT ANGRY, BUT WHO ARE YOU TO KNOW WHAT IS RIGHT OR WRONG. WHAT IS AND WHAT SHOULD BE. TO TINKER WITH THE FATE OF ONE INDIVIDUAL COULD DESTROY THE WORLD

WE HAVE OUR OWN KIND OF MERCY, BOY

A SHARP EDGE

AND RELIABILITY IS IMPORTANT TOO, OF COURSE

AH, YES, YOU TRIED TO WARN PRINCESS KELI

SORRY

A HUNDRED AND SEVEN, NOT BAD, EH, UP YOURS BONEY

YES, YOU DEFINITELY HAD ME WORRIED FOR A MOMENT, THERE

YOU WAIT 'TILL THAT SOPPY LOT FIND OUT I'VE LEFT ALL ME MONEY TO THE CAT

WHAT CAN PEOPLE RELY ON, BOY? NOT ON LOVE, NOT ON PEOPLE, NOT ON GODS. BUT ON ME.

I AM THE SURCEASE OF PAIN. I AM THE LOVER OF THE UNLOVED AND THE COMPANION OF THE LONELY. I REUNITE THE PARTED AND END ALL SORROW

I AM THE ULTIMATE REALITY

ON ME, BOY, THEY CAN RELY

SNAP!

uh... CAN ANYONE SELL ME A **VERY** FAST HORSE ...?

WHAT A PIECE OF **LUCK**!...

...WE HAPPEN TO BE **VERY** FAST HORSE SALESMEN!

WE KEEP 'EM IN THAT **VERY** DARK ALLEY OVER THERE

I DON'T SEE ANY HOR...

...SES

25

HOW'D I DO **THAT**?

UM...CAN ANYONE SELL ME A HORSE?

A QUIET EVENING, ALBERT, NO PROBLEMS HERE. BUT IT'S A SHAME ABOUT THE PRINCESS, SO... YOUNG...

YOU ALL RIGHT, MASTER?

YES, YES, OF COURSE. IT'S JUST ...SAD

MASTER?

I SHALL SEND THE BOY...

CHEEKY YOUNG DEVIL, HIM

BECAUSE I SHALL HAVE...

I HAVE A STRANGE CRAVING FOR...

...A NIGHT OFF

FUN!

TO GOODIE HAMSTRING...

FOR THE HORS?

I WON'T BE A MINUTE

JUST PUTTING IN THE BIT ABOUT SOUND MIND AND BODY... DAMNED NONSENSE

HOW DO YOU... ...I MEAN... HOW DO YOU KNOW WHO I AM !?

'CAUSE I'M A BLOODY OL' WITCH, THAT'S HOW

SHALL I NEED MY SHAWL?

NAH... IT'S PROBABLY PRETTY WARM WHERE I'M GOING

COME ON I AIN'T GOT ALL NIGHT

I'M DOING THIS ALL WRONG

ARE YOU? I WOULDN'T KNOW

I'VE NEVER... DONE THIS BEFORE

ME NEITHER

WE CAN LEARN TOGETHER

NOW...

IS THAT YOU?

IT'S WHO I'VE ALWAYS BEEN

BUT I HAVE TO TAKE YOUR...

I'M STAYING HERE

TAKE CARE MORT

YOU MAY WANT TO HANG ON TO YOUR JOB...

...BUT WILL YOU EVER BE ABLE TO LET GO?

THE ABBOT LOBSANG, 54TH ABBOT OF THE LISTENING MONKS

MMMMMMMMMMMMM

...AND ALL THE OTHER 53, TOO...

AH, THERE YOU ARE. WHAT HAPPENED TO THE USUAL CHAP?

USUAL CHAP?

YES, TALL THIN... DOESN'T GET ENOUGH TO EAT...

...ER... ...HE SENT ME... ...ER... ...YOU'VE MET DEATH BEFORE?

OH, YEAH. I'M VERY EXPERIENCED AT DYING

OH, I SEE. REINCARNATION!

RIGHT. BUT I WOULDN'T DO IT IF I HAD MY TIME ALL OVER AGAIN

DROP ME OFF NEAR THE VILLAGE. I'M BEING CONCEIVED AGAIN ABOUT NOW...

...THE SCENERY'S NOT MUCH, BUT I DO GET NINE MONTHS IN THE WARM. BEST OF LUCK IN THE NEW JOB, ANYWAY...

I EXPECT YOU **CAN'T** **WAIT** TO GET OUT THERE AGAIN, EH?

...ALBERT TELLS ME **SOMEONE** HAS BEEN **TAKING BOOKS** OUT OF THE **LIBRARY**...

...BOOKS ABOUT THE **LIVES** OF YOUNG PEOPLE...

YOUNG GIRLS, IN FACT... NOW WE WERE ALL YOUN... ONCE SOME OF US...

...BUT THIS **MUST STOP**. YES?

YES, ER, THAT IS, I...

JOLLY GOOD. NOW THEN...

ER...

...YES...

RIGHT...

...WHY NOT LET YSABELL SHOW YOU THE GARDEN?

BUT I'VE **ALREADY** SEEN...

COME ON...

41

HE **LET** ME GROW UP...

...BUT THERE'S NO **REAL** TIME HERE...

...I'VE BEEN **SIXTEEN** FOR **THIRTY-TWO** YEARS

I WANT SOME **REAL** LIFE!

I **COMMAND** SOMEONE TO **NOTICE** ME!

TFK, TFK! I KNOW FWHAT **YOU** NEED!

LIFE'S SOMETHING I JUST READ ABOUT

IT'S SOMETHING I TAKE AWAY

NOT VERY EFFICIENTLY. YOU SAID YOU'VE CHANGED HISTORY

I DIDN'T ASK FOR THIS JOB, YOU KNOW

YOU'LL HAVE TO TELL FATHER...

AH, THERE'S YOUR PROBLEM...

YES?

...YOU'RE DEAD...

PEOPLE THINK YOU'RE DEAD. THE WORLD THINKS YOU'RE DEAD...

I'M NOT DEAD!

...YOUR OPINION DOESN'T COUNT

THE FIRST THING YOU LEARN AT U.U. IS THAT PEOPLE DON'T PAY MUCH ATTENTION TO WHAT'S TRUE

ACTUALLY THE FIRST THING IS WHERE THE LAVATORIES ARE, BUT YOU KNOW WHAT I MEAN...

BUT YOU CAN SEE ME...

AH, THAT'S BECAUSE I'M A WIZARD. WE KNOW ABOUT THESE THINGS

43

44

HI! HOW'RE YOU DOING?

IT HELPS IF YOU THINK OF IT AS THE LAST DAY OF THE REST OF YOUR LIFE

YOU, SIR, YOU HAVE A LUCKY FACE...

OH, **NO**...

HISTORY IS HARDER TO GET RID OF THAN **NUCLEAR WASTE**. HISTORY IS A RAKE IN THE **GRASS**. HISTORY SPRINGS BACK INTO SHAPE LIKE AN OLD SWEATER ...RECLAIMING ITS OWN

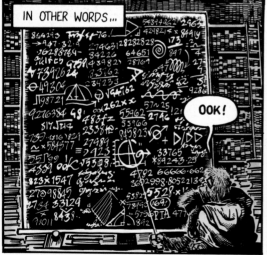

IN OTHER WORDS...

OOK!

I'LL HAVE A **DRINK**, AND THEN EVERYTHING WILL BE BETTER

"..MUTTERMUTTERMUTTERMUTTER.."

EXCUSE ME, WHAT DO PEOPLE **DRINK** AROUND HERE?

WELL, ZUR, AROUND HERE UZ DO DRINK **SCUMBLE**

YURR, **SCUMBLE!**

OH. RIGHT. A **PINT** OF **SCUMBLE**, THEN, PLEASE

A **PINT?**

CHEERS!

CHEERS..!

VERY NICE,
VERY **FRUITY**.
CAN I HAVE
ANOTHER ?

ER, YEAH,
US KNOWS
WHAT GOES INTO
GOOD SCUMBLE
ROUND HERE

...THAT'S
WHY US DRINKS
GIN AND TONIC...

ANOTHER
PINT ?

YUR, 'AS 'E
BEEN PUTTIN'
WATER IN THE
SCUMBLE ?

TALK SENSE.
EVERYONE D'KNOW
WHAT HAPPENS IF
YOU LETS **WATER**
TOUCH SCUMBLE

OH, NO !
IT'S COMI
THROUG
THE WAL

WHAT **SHOULD BE** BEARS DOWN...

...ON WHAT **IS**

WHEN IT CLOSES UP... WILL SHE **DIE**?

YOU'RE THINKING THE WRONG WAY. SHE **WILL HAVE BEEN** DEAD. FOR DAYS I THINK.

ALL OF THIS WON'T HAVE HAPPENED

YOU'RE A WIZARD. **DO** SOMETHING!

GOOD GRIEF, **NO-ONE'S** GOT THAT KIND OF POWER **NOW**

BACK IN THE OLD DAYS, MAYBE. SOMEONE LIKE OLD **MALICH** HERE KNEW SOME REALLY HUGE SPELLS. MOST POWERFUL WIZARD WHO EVER LIVED, THEY SAID

BUT **THAT'S**...

...HEY, WHAT HAPPENED TO HIM?

WHO KNOWS?

ONE DAY— FAZAAM!

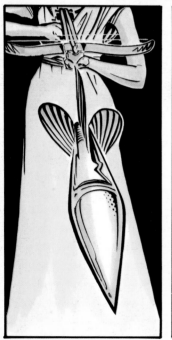

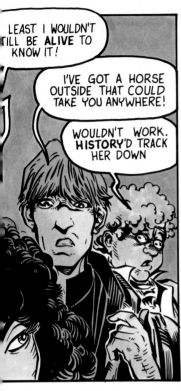

LEAST I WOULDN'T TILL BE **ALIVE** TO KNOW IT!

I'VE GOT A HORSE OUTSIDE THAT COULD TAKE YOU ANYWHERE!

WOULDN'T WORK. **HISTORY'D** TRACK HER DOWN

I SHALL BE CROWNED. AT **DAWN**, DAY AFTER TOMORROW

DAWN? WHY DAWN?

IT'S THE EARLIEST IT CAN BE ARRANGED. ALL THAT PROTOCOL, YOU KNOW. AHAHAHA...

BUT THAT'S WHEN THE HISTORIES **COLLIDE!**

THEN I SHALL SHOW THE WORLD HOW A REAL QUEEN CAN DIE

BUT I **KNOW** HOW QUEENS DIE! THEY DIE LIKE EVERYONE ELSE!

CAN MAGIC HELP? **MALICH'S** MAGIC?

MAYBE. BUT HE NEVER WROTE **ANYTHING** DOWN—

EVERYONE HAS **ONE** BOOK IN THEM

I'LL BE BACK!

WHY DOESN'T HE USE THE DAMN DOOR!

"...SCRITCH, SCRITCH...SCRITCH..."

UP THERE!

IS IT ALBERT'S BOOK?

SORT OF...

...IT'S ALBERT'S SHELF

HE'S ALBERTO MALICH!

HE SHOULD HAVE DIED THOUSANDS OF YEARS AGO!

"IT'S THEIR FAULT MASTER AIN'T BACK!" THOUGHT ALBERT AS HE CREPT THROUGH THE STACK, "I'LL TEACH 'EM A LESSON, THE YOUNG—"

I'M READING WHAT HE'S DOING ...NOW!

ALBERT!

YOU **ARE** ALBERT MALICH YOU WERE THE GREATEST I NEED YOUR HELP—

IN THE DREGS OF THE NIGHT

NOTHIN' DOIN'!

I DON'T SHEE THE POINT

SORRY?

WHAT IS SHUPPOSED TO HAPPEN?

HOW MANY HAVE YOU HAD?

FORTY-SHEVEN

JUST ABOU ANYTHING

THEY ALL HATE ME, YOU KNOW. I HAVE NO FRIENDSH

EVEYONE SHOULD HAVE FRIENDS

I THINK...

...I THINK I COULD BE FRIENDSH WITH THAT GREEN BOTTLE...

...OF THE FUTURE...

LONELINESS...

...SADNESS...

MORT!

MORT, FATHER'S GONE!

I...KNOW

IT'S **YOUR** FAULT! YOU'VE BEEN PUTTING IDEAS INTO HIS HEAD! **TIME OFF** — PAH!

SO? LET EVERYONE LIVE A BIT LONGER

READ.

MORT, I REALLY THINK YOU'RE GOING TOO—

SHALL I ASK YOU AGAIN?

'—ALBERT LOOKED INTO MORT'S EYES AND SAW NO PITY AND KNEW THAT THIS **NEW** DEATH WOULD **HUNT** HIM DOWN AND TAKE HIM TO THOSE **DARK STARS** WHERE...'

THERE'S JUST A ROW OF DOTS, MORT! JUST DOT, DOT, DOT!

THAT'S 'COS IT DON'T DARE WRITE IT! **THEY'LL** BE WAITIN'!

I DAREN'T DIE!

WHAT **THEY**?

THINGS WITHOUT FACES! YOU MAKE POWERFUL ENEMIES, WIZARDING!

BUT **THIS** IS LIFE? THE SAME DAY, OVER AND OVER AGAIN? TIME STRETCHED OUT THIN? THIS IS JUST—**NOTHING**!

THERE WAS AN ARRANGEMENT!

NOT WITH ME.

HARGA'S HOUSE of RIBS

HARGA'S HOUSE OF RIBS...A GREASY SPOON

THAT'S DOUBLE BACON, SAUS—

AFTER YOU EAT PLEASE WASH YOUR HANDS

HOW'D YOU DO THAT?

TIME IS NOT IMPORTANT

HAPPINESS...

...FOR OTHERS, NATURALLY...

...IT'S SHORT...

DON'T THINK OF THIS AS AN ENDING.

WOULD YOU LIKE A SANDWICH?

HOW MANY IS THAT?

ONE HUNDRED AND SEVENTEEN

TOO SLOW!

YOU HORRIBLE LOT! WELL, YOU'RE GOING TO DO SOME REAL MAGIC—

COO?

— YOU'RE GOING TO SUMMON DEATH!

BUM!

THE·RITE·OF
ASHKENTE

TO SUMMON DEATH:
TAKE THREE SMALL PIECES OF WOOD
AND 2CC OF MOUSE BLOOD. AND
BAGS OF STYLE...

BURIED ALIVE!

I SUPPOSE DEAD KINGS LIKE COMPANY

THAT'S SO UNFAIR!

THERE'S NO JUSTICE

THERE'S JUST ME

THAT'S WHAT FATHER ALWAYS SAYS

I KNOW

I HAVE FINISHED MY APPRENTICESHIP

AND I GAVE HIM A WORTHWHILE CAREER

COMMUNITY SERVICE, ALMOST

WELL, ENOUGH IS ENOUGH

COME, ALBERT

NO, NO, I'VE DECIDED TO STAY

THEY **NEED** ME HERE!

DON'T LET US KEEP YOU—

SORRY YOU'RE LEAVING—

CALL AGAIN WHEN YOU'VE LESS TIME—

BUT I NEED YOU, ALBERT. YOU MAKE ME LAUGH. COME!

LOOK AFTER THIS...

...ITS NAME IS SCAMP

TOO LATE...

OF COURSE I KNOW WHAT TO DO, BOY...MM ...DEARLY BELOVED, WE ARE...THAT IS, SOME OF US...GATHERED HERE TODAY...

WHERE'S THAT DAMN ELEPHANT?

I THINK WE NEED GO NO FURTHER...

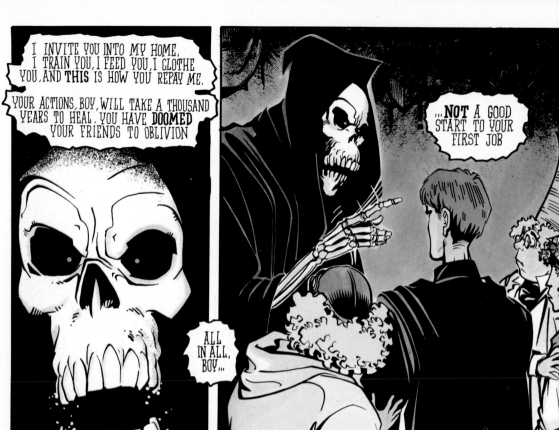

BATTLE COMMENCES...

...WITH SIDE EFFECTS...

SOME DAYS LATER...

AND WHO, MM, GIVES THIS WOMAN IN MATRIMONY?

ER. ME?

THE RECEPTION...

HELLO

WE THOUGHT YOU WEREN'T COMING

THERE WAS A SMALL WAR ON, YOU KNOW HOW IT IS WHEN YOU'RE TRYING TO GET AWAY

ER. THANK YOU FOR THE TOAST RACK

THAT WAS FROM ALBERT

LOOK, I'VE GOT TO KNOW!

WHAT HAPPENED..?

...ONE MINUTE WE WERE FIGHTING, THE NEXT...

...WE WERE ALL HERE! NOW SHE'S MADE ME A DUKE! EVERYTHING'S **RIGHT!**

HOW D
YOU D
THAT

WELL, THEY DO SAY **DEATH** CHANGES THINGS

...HAD TO WORK MY FINGERS TO THE BONE

BUT DON'T THINK YOU'VE GOT AWAY WITH ANYTHING, IT'S A HARD JOB, DUKING, **YOU'VE** GOT TO MAKE HISTORY

I'VE GOT TO MAKE IT WORK?

YOU'VE GOT TO MAKE IT WORK **DIFFERENTLY**

AND NO-ONE HAS TO DIE?

OH, EVERYONE HAS TO DIE. JUST NOT YE